Packed with splendiferous pictures →

← Horace is historical and hysterical.

FIVE REASONS WHY YOU'LL LOVE HORACE AND HARRIET.

There's a pigeon called Barry. ←

Harriet is amazing and you'll want to be her friend! →

WHO'S WHO

Horace

Harriet
(that's me)

Barry

Grandad

Mayor Silverbottom

Duke Cuthbert Emery Buckington Silverbottom II (or Cuthbert, for short)

Fraser

Megan

← Fabtastic friends! →

Angela Spicklicket

Mum

WHERE'S WHERE

Mayor Silverbottom's House

My house

School

Princes Park

DOGGY AEROBICS!

TRAIN STATION

CINEMA

LIBRARY

BRIM

Museum

Cinema

BRIM

BANK

BRIM

BRIM

raser's
House

Megan's
House

The Brim

For Mum and Dad, for Absolutely Everything.

OXFORD
UNIVERSITY PRESS

Great Clarendon Street, Oxford OX2 6DP
Oxford University Press is a department of the University of Oxford.
It furthers the University's objective of excellence in research, scholarship,
and education by publishing worldwide. Oxford is a registered trade mark
of Oxford University Press in the UK and in certain other countries

Copyright © Clare Elsom 2018
Illustrations © Clare Elsom 2018

The moral rights of the author have been asserted

Database right Oxford University Press (maker)

First published 2018

British Library Cataloguing in Publication Data

Data available

ISBN: 978-0-19-275874-3

1 3 5 7 9 10 8 6 4 2

Printed in China

Paper used in the production of this book is a natural,
recyclable product made from wood grown in sustainable forests.
The manufacturing process conforms to the environmental
regulations of the country of origin.

HORACE & Harriet

Take on the Town

WRITTEN AND ILLUSTRATED
BY THE SPLENDIFEROUS

CLARE ELSOM

OXFORD
UNIVERSITY PRESS

Fine hat

Curly
moustache

Very shiny
medals

~~Rather~~
~~large tummy~~

Lord Commander Horatio Frederick
Wallington Nincompoop Maximus
Pimpleberry the Third

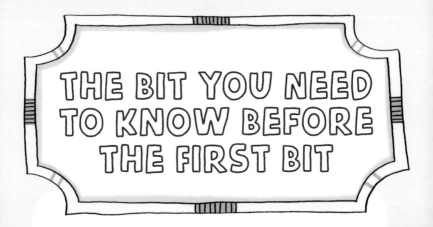

THE BIT YOU NEED TO KNOW BEFORE THE FIRST BIT

This is Lord Commander Horatio Frederick Wallington Nincompoop Maximus Pimpleberry the Third.

He is a statue in Princes Park. He has a fine hat, a curly moustache, very shiny medals, and a rather large tummy (although I shouldn't really mention that last bit—my mum says it's rude to comment on people's tummies).

1

I walk past Lord Commander Horatio
Frederick Wallington Nincompoop Maximus

Pimpleberry the
Third all the time,
and, let me tell you,
it doesn't look much
fun being a statue.

He is always being
pooed on by pigeons.

Lord Commander Horatio Frederick
Wallington Nincompoop Maximus
Pimpleberry the Third

AND being covered
in graffiti.
AND having practical
jokes played on him.
AND getting litter
dumped around him.

AND having people sit on him to have
boring phone conversations and eat boring
sandwiches.

And did I mention the *pigeon poo*?

3

I asked my grandad why the statue was there (Grandad knows *everything*), and he said that hundreds of years ago—so far back that it would make your brain all swirly and your eyes all boggly to even think about that much time ago—Lord Commander Horatio Frederick Wallington Nincompoop Maximus Pimpleberry the Third had lived in our town and had won the most fierce and terrifying battle there ever was.

The battle was between Lord Commander Horatio Frederick Wallington Nincompoop Maximus Pimpleberry the Third and his dastardly enemy, Duke Cuthbert Emery Buckington Silverbottom the Second.

 5

Grandad said that the battle involved
hurling a lot of custard pies, eggs, water
bombs, and cowpats, which sounded quite
fun, and not terrifying at all, if you ask me.

Lord Commander Horatio Frederick Wallington Nincompoop Maximus Pimpleberry the Third won the battle, defeating Duke Cuthbert Emery Buckington Silverbottom the Second by several cowpats and at least five custard pies, and that's why he is now a statue in Princes Park.

Apparently Duke Cuthbert Emery Buckington Silverbottom the Second also has a statue, but it's on the other side of town, in front of the Silverbottom mansion. The Silverbottom family are still around today, you see—in fact, one of them is the mayor of our town. Mayor Silverbottom is NOT a very nice man. But more about that later.

Oh, and I'm Harriet, by the way.

 8

Me, Harri!

My friends, like my BEST friends Fraser and Megan, sometimes call me Harri. So does Grandad.

Mum tends to call me 'poppet' and 'sweetykins', but she's a mum so I guess she's allowed.

People like Angela Spicklicket and her giggling gang, who have been mean to me ever since I beat them at Sports Day, call me all sorts of things. I'd rather they didn't speak

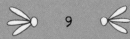

to me at all.

So, anyway, that's some important stuff to know, and now we can get on with the First Bit, and that's where the story *really* starts ...

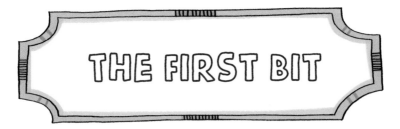

THE FIRST BIT

It was a Saturday, and I decided to go to Princes Park to practise Going to the Park on My Own.

Mum said I could Go to the Park on My Own when I was ten.

Which I'm not.

I'm seven.

And a quarter.

Which meant that Grandad was with me, but, as instructed, he was walking AT LEAST thirty steps behind me, so that I could practise.

I was looking across the ornamental lake

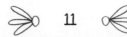

to where the statue of Lord Commander
Horatio Frederick Wallington Nincompoop
Maximus Pimpleberry the Third stood.
Somebody had cleaned the graffiti and
pigeon poo off him, but some older kids
were now throwing empty cans and trying
to hit the traffic cone
that was currently
wedged on his
head. They
soon got bored
and wandered
away.

And THAT was when it happened.

Lord Commander Horatio Frederick
Wallington Nincompoop Maximus
Pimpleberry the Third …

got down from his pillar, and walked away.

(Actually, he stamped his foot, shouted something that would get him in SERIOUS TROUBLE with Mum, and *then* got down from his pillar. But anyway.)

I looked around for Grandad and saw he was

Lord Commander Horatio Frederick Wallington Nincompoop Maximus Pimpleberry the Third safely occupied Daydreaming About the Old Times on a bench, so I crept around the lake to have a closer look. The statue was hopping around next to his pillar and trying to yank the traffic cone from his head. I couldn't believe it. Well, have you ever seen a statue come to life, start talking, and GET DOWN from its pillar? No. Exactly.

14

'That is QUITE ENOUGH OF THIS NONSENSE!' he was yelling. '*Nobody* should treat Lord Commander Horatio Frederick Wallington Nincompoop Maximus Pimpleberry the Third, winner of illustrious battles, thrice world champion of the international egg-and-spoon race, and the largest and most brilliant statue in Princes Park, in this most *disgraceful manner!*'

The statue puffed out his chest and straightened his medals. 'I demand a better place to reside. Henceforth it is *time*—' he paused for dramatic effect '—for some INVADING!' Then he whipped out a telescope and peered around the park. 'Aha!' he exclaimed, pointing the telescope towards the lake, even though he was standing right next to it. 'Target spotted!

Just the place! And there's even a ship!'
he said excitedly. 'A little below the usual
standards, but it will have to suffice.'

Lord Commander Horatio Frederick
Wallington Nincompoop Maximus
Pimpleberry the Third clambered into the
pedalo and began pedalling furiously across
the lake, waving some twigs threateningly
at the ducks.

'Barry, go forth and warn them of our
impending invasion!' He said this last bit to
a pigeon that had been perched on his pillar.

Barry the Pigeon looked rather unimpressed at this command and lazily flapped his way back to the bank. I was watching all this with my mouth hanging open. I was also pretty sure the pedalo was starting to sink.

The statue seemed to think so too.

'Abandon ship! Abandon ship!' he yelled in alarm. 'You dastardly swines!' he shouted at the ducks. 'You filthy fiends!

You have sabotaged my ship! Barry, come hither and help!'

I decided I should intervene. And found myself talking *to a statue*.

'*Excuse* me,' I said, in my Extra Polite Voice, 'are you stuck …?'

Lord Commander Horatio

Frederick Wallington Nincompoop
Maximus Pimpleberry the Third swung
around and stared at me.

'I *think*,' I continued,
'that you are too heavy
to be in a pedalo.
You should
probably
get out
before you sink
it completely. The lake's shallow; you can
just walk back.'

He peered doubtfully over the side and
carefully tested the water with his toe.

'By Jove, you're right!' he exclaimed,
as he waded back to the bank. 'Sterling
efforts, boy!'

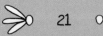

Boy?

He came over and stuck out his hand for me to shake. 'Lord Commander Horatio Frederick Wallington Nincompoop Maximus Pimpleberry the Third, winner of illustrious battles, thrice world champion of the international egg-and-spoon race, and the largest and most brilliant statue in Princes Park, although presently in search of a new home, pleased to make your acquaintance.'

I shook his hand. 'Ouch!' I yelped. It was like having your hand crushed by a rock. Because he was a statue.

'And this is my second in command, Barry.' He gestured fondly to the pigeon. 'The only pigeon in Princes Park never to

have fouled me.'

'Er, hello Barry,' I said. And now I was talking to a pigeon. 'Um, I'm not a boy,' I told the statue. 'I'm a girl!

My name is Harriet. You can call me Harri.'

'A girl!' he scoffed. 'Where, might I enquire, is your long hair? Your skirt? Your parasol?'

'My *para-what*? I absolutely AM a girl! I don't have to wear skirts and have long hair,' I said, and crossed my arms, because I was cross.

He looked suspicious. 'Harri, you say? A ludicrous name!'

I gawped at him. He was one to talk! 'Me? What about *you*? Surely you shorten your name?'

He sniffed. 'I *may*, on the *odd occasion*, have been known to answer to Horace.'

'Horace,' I repeated. Much better. 'What were you doing, anyway?' I asked.

 24

'I was undertaking an invasion of
Duck Island, yonder!' Horace answered.
'I require a new residence. My pillar has
become too unsatisfactory for such a *fine*
statue as myself.'

I stared at him. 'You were trying to
invade the duck house? That's ridiculous.
You can't live there!'

It was at that point I noticed that people in the park were beginning to point at us. I saw Grandad walking towards us with his 'Now What Are You Doing?' look on his face.

I was talking to a statue, after all. And a pigeon. And Horace was hopping around, waving twigs at the ducks.

Suddenly the park attendant appeared on the opposite side of the lake, and he began to hop around too, when he saw his capsized pedalo.

'Look,' I said decisively to Horace, 'you clearly need some help. Why don't you come with me and Grandad? I'm sure we've got somewhere you can stay while we decide what on *earth* to do with you.'

Horace looked around. 'You are offering me your castle? How noble! Very well, Strange Girl, let me take a look and see if it appears satisfactory.'

'*Castle*? I never said anything about a castle! And my name is HARRIET.'

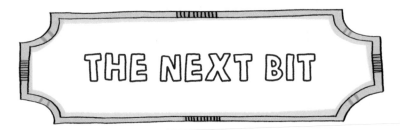

On the way home from the park

I introduced Grandad to Horace.

Thankfully, they seemed to hit it off.

Grandad will talk to anyone. He used to

be in the navy, and he and Horace spent

most of the time comparing medals that

they'd won In the Olden Days.

Barry the Pigeon came along too.

Horace was amazed at EVERYTHING
— at cars, at adverts, at people's shoes,
at scooters … Frankly it was a bit
embarrassing. But I guess if you've been
stuck on a pillar for hundreds of years, you
might not have seen very much outside
the park.

While Horace was busy quizzing a
terrified Mrs Patel from Number 12 about
her lawnmower, I explained to Grandad
that Horace was tired of the pigeon poo
and graffiti and traffic cones and litter in
the park, and that he needed somewhere

to stay.

'Hmm. What about our shed?' whispered Grandad to me.

This was *exactly* what I'd been thinking. Grandad was brilliant like that.

We managed to sneak Horace down the side of our house and into the back garden without most of our Nosy Neighbours noticing.

I'm pretty sure Mrs Crawley at Number 63 saw us, but she notices EVERYTHING. And also Horace wanted to have a go on the swing in her front garden, which didn't help matters.

'Er, perhaps I'll go and mention to your mum that it's best not to use the garden this evening …' Grandad said, and

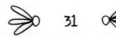

he disappeared into our house.

***

Horace spluttered with outrage when he saw the shed.

'Peculiar Child, THIS is NOT a fit property for Lord Commander Horatio Frederick Wallington Nincompoop Maximus Pimpleberry the Third,' he said.

'My *name* is Harriet. H-a-r-r-i-e-t,' I said through gritted teeth, saying it e-x-t-r-a s-l-o-w-l-y. 'You were happy with a duck house not long ago!' I reminded him. 'The shed is super cosy; Grandad and I hang out in there all the time. And I certainly can't bring you into the house. Mum would have a fit!'

I glanced through the back window and

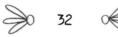

saw Mum practising an exercise routine in the kitchen. Mum is a bit of a fitness freak, and she's even started her own aerobics class for dogs. Yes, really.

I turned back to Horace. 'Look, you can't wander around out here on your own: goodness knows what you'll get up to. Invade the bird box, probably.'

Barry raised an eyebrow at that idea.

'You shall not boss me around like this, you young whippersnapper!' retorted Horace.

I wasn't sure what a whippersnapper was. It sounded like some sort of fish. He really was a bit of a rude statue.

'Well, you clearly need somewhere to stay, and I don't see anyone else offering

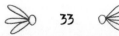

to help you!' I told him, getting cross. 'And
I'm not that young: I'm seven and
a quarter, I'll have you know. How old
are *you*?'

Mum had often told me I shouldn't ask
grown-ups how old they were because it
was rude, but as he'd just called
me a fish, I decided I
should be allowed
this time.

'387 years!' said
Horace. 'And a half.'
Hmm. That was
pretty old.
I stared at
Horace. Horace stared
right back. Now, I'm usually

excellent at staring competitions: I beat Fraser and Megan all the time. But it turns out that out-staring a statue is really rather difficult. However, I am VERY obstinate and it came in useful here.

Horace threw up his hands in defeat. 'Fine. For ONE evening, I shall reside in the dwelling you call "The Shed". But tomorrow, tomorrow we search for a new home—the finest home in all the land!'

With that, he marched off into the shed, waving his telescope.

I marched off towards the house for my tea. I didn't have a telescope to wave, so I just crossed my arms with a *Hrmph!* sound to show him I had NEARLY HAD ENOUGH OF HIS BEHAVIOUR.

What on earth had I got myself into?

THE THIRD BIT

The next morning I woke up to a strange sound.

Tap. Tap-tap-tap. Taptaptaptap.

I opened my eyes and wondered why there was a pigeon tapping at my bedroom

window. Then I wondered why I felt
nervous and my tummy was all squiggly.
Then I remembered. There was a rather
demanding statue called Horace hiding in
our garden shed.

I groaned and looked out of the window.
And my mouth fell open. I flung on my
dressing gown and dashed into the garden.

Property of
Lord Commander
Horatio Frederick
Wellington Noncompoop
Maximus Pimpleberry
the Third

'*Horace!*' I hissed at the shed. 'What

have you done?'

Horace's face popped around the door. 'A

good morning to you, Curious Youngster!

 39

Why, I made my shed better,' he said.

'You're meant to be HIDING!' I groaned. 'And it's not your shed; it's Grandad's!'

'Well, 'tis mine now,' said Horace. 'I've invaded it.'

'Would you *please* stop invading things?' I sighed.

Horace clambered up to the crow's nest and looked out at the view.

'I dare say one could be happy here after all,' declared Horace. 'A solid construction, fine views, cannons in place …'

Suddenly I froze, as I heard the back door opening—I *really* didn't want Mum to see what Horace had done. She liked the garden to have A Calming Atmosphere so

 40

she could do her yoga, and I was pretty sure Horace and the new Cannon Shed wouldn't be very calming.

Luckily, it was Grandad.

'Ah,' he said, looking at the shed and stroking his chin thoughtfully.

'I *know*,' I said, wringing my hands in panic. 'What do we—?'

'Is that a round-shot demi-culverin you've put in there, Horace?' Grandad interrupted, gesturing at a cannon.

I gawped at him. A round-shot *what*?

Horace looked delighted. 'Why, sir, indeed it is! A marvellous observation. I would be thrilled to offer a fellow man-at-arms a tour, if it would please you?'

Before I knew what was happening,

Horace was showing Grandad around
the shed and they were reminiscing about
their time in the navy again.

'Incredible,' chuckled Grandad
admiringly. 'My shed has never looked
so good!' He patted me on the back as he
walked back to the house. 'You're certainly
going to have a job getting him to go back
to his pillar, Harri.'

I gulped. I had a feeling that Going Back
to the Pillar wasn't Horace's plan at all.

And how had this become *my* problem?

THE FOURTH BIT

Horace was back in the crow's nest, scanning the horizon through his telescope.

'I declare,' said Horace, 'that my shed must surely be the finest dwelling in … HANG on a moment.'

He paused and focused his telescope. 'Ho! I am wrong: a finer home has been located! My Acquiescent Aide, to whom does THAT dwelling belong?'

I sighed and carefully climbed up.

'That's Mayor Silverbottom's home!' I exclaimed, peering through the telescope.

'You're right, it's the poshest house in the town. Have you heard of him? The Silverbottoms are … Oh.'

Oops. I suddenly remembered the story about Horace's worst enemy. At first I thought he hadn't heard me …

'GALLOPING GARGOYLES!' Horace exploded.

… but then it was clear that he probably had.

'FIZZLING FERRETS! Jabbering jackdaws! Mayor *Silverbottom*?' Horace spluttered in fury. 'Is this mayor of yours a descendant of my dastardly arch-enemy, Cuthbert?'

'Um, yes,' I said. 'There's, er, a statue of Cuthbert in front of the house, I think.'

I peered at the house again. Sure enough, there was a statue that looked a bit similar to Horace … only taller and thinner. (I thought I wouldn't mention that bit.)

'UTTERLY PREPOSTEROUS!' bellowed Horace. 'What madness is this? How has a Silverbottom come to live in an

 46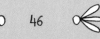

ENORMOUS HOUSE and be the mayor?'

'Keep your voice down!' I begged. The

Nosy Neighbours were probably having a

great time.

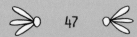

'Those fiendish crooks. Rogues, the lot
of them!' seethed Horace. 'We'll see about
this. Barry, prepare for an
imminent invasion!'

'What do you mean?'
I asked in alarm.

'I will not reside here
while Cuthbert's descendants
occupy *that* establishment.
I thenceforth claim the
Silverbottom mansion as my new
home. We must prepare to occupy
it immediately!'

We?

I stared as Horace clambered down from
the crow's nest. 'Wait, Horace, we can't do
that!'

Although … it was quite tempting. Part of me wanted to do something a bit nasty to Mayor Silverbottom, as he was a HORRIBLE person. When he visited our school, Oliver Anderson from Year 6 asked him if his bottom was actually made out of silver, which is a PERFECTLY reasonable question and really quite funny. But the mayor was so cross when we all laughed that he made us miss our lunch to write an apology! He also closed down the swimming pool that had all the cool water slides. I think he kept it for his private use. *And* he stopped the local shops selling chocolate biscuits for his latest healthy living campaign. Can you imagine? NO CHOCOLATE BISCUITS.

But even so, you can't just invade someone's house!

'Why?' asked Horace. 'What's the worst that could happen, Nervous Maiden?'

'Well, we might get spotted on the security cameras! Mayor Silverbottom might report us to the police … or my *mum*!' I said, horrified. 'He might set his guard dogs on us! He might—'

Horace stopped in his tracks. 'D–dogs …? Dogs, you say?'

'Yes!' I insisted. 'He has loads of them!'

Horace made a funny squeaking noise, and then hurriedly cleared his throat. 'Ah. Right.'

I looked at him curiously. 'Are you afraid of dogs, Horace?'

'ABSOLUTELY not, no, not at all.
Not afraid of anything. Ha, NO. *No,*' said
Horace, straightening his hat.

I glanced at Barry, who was nodding
behind Horace's back.

I decided this might be my only chance.

'Horace, there are definitely going to
be some other
places in this
town that
are entirely
dog-free and
less—um—
Owned by
the Mayor.
Why don't
we just have

a look? I'm sure we can find somewhere even better than the Silverbottom mansion!'

Horace looked torn. 'Better, you say?'

'Much better,' I said decisively.

'Well … obviously I am not troubled by a mere hound or two, but if there were somewhere better, then let us find it without further ado!'

THE MIDDLE BIT

I got changed into my favourite old
T-shirt and jeans and told Grandad that I
was going with Horace to find him a new
place to live. Grandad said that was OK,
but Horace had to look after me, and we
had to be careful crossing roads and be
back in time for tea.

Horace took this very seriously, and they saluted each other a lot.

I privately thought I might be the one looking after Horace.

'Foot soldiers, assemble!' Horace ordered, looking at me and Barry. 'Let us see what this town has to offer. Forward, march!' And he strode off towards the town centre.

I had the feeling I was in for a *lonnggg* day.

The museum was one of the first places we walked past, and Horace peered up at the huge brick building, looking impressed. 'I say! A grand entrance, majestic columns … and look how many townsfolk will get the chance to admire me!' he mused, watching the crowds entering the museum. 'Yes! I rather like the idea of living here.'

We went into the biggest gallery and Horace struck a dignified pose.

However, the visitors all seemed much more interested in the dinosaurs than Horace.

'Inadequate!' Horace shouted grumpily,

after being ignored for half an hour, and he stormed out of the museum.

He knocked over a vase on the way out, but it was old and broken, so I'm pretty sure it wasn't worth anything.

Next we inspected the cinema, which is in a really cool building. Horace didn't really know what a cinema was, so we

DO NOT TOUCH
(MAY BITE)

went inside. I used the last of my pocket
money on tickets for me and Barry. Horace
got in for free because he was 387 years
old. He seemed amazed by the cinema
screen, and it was only the adverts! THEN
I realized the 3D movie was all about dogs
and suddenly Horace seemed a teeny bit
less keen.

So that was no good either.

***

We attracted a lot of attention as we walked along. I'd got pretty used to Horace by now, but I guess other people weren't. They did a lot of staring. Horace waved back.

'The townsfolk attire themselves rather
strangely, do they not?' Horace whispered
to me, in a voice that wasn't really a
whisper at all, but more like a shout. 'Why

is nobody wearing hats and medals?'

'Because *no one* wears hats and medals! They probably don't have any,' I whispered back, in a voice that was *actually* a whisper.

'These poor people! They must feel terribly envious of me,' said Horace. 'Hold fast, my young compatriot, *this* is the mansion we are seeking!'

We were outside the library.

'Ye-e-es,' I said warily, 'but, Horace, if we go inside you have to—'

'GREETINGS, FELLOW CITIZENS!' Horace boomed, as he walked through the doors.

Oh dear.

I dashed in behind him. 'Horace! You

 60

have to keep quiet!' I whispered

frantically at him.

He gazed around in wonder.

'Zarbles! Just LOOK at all these

tomes!'

'Shh!' hissed the librarian, frowning

at us.

I cringed. 'Horace, I don't think this is *quite* the place for you ...'

'Incredible,' mused Horace, staring at the shelves. 'Volumes on art, science, ultimate frisbee—whatever that might be. They must have hundreds of books about me!'

The librarian came over to us. 'Really, sir, will you *please* keep your voice down!' she scolded Horace. 'And no pets allowed in here!' She glared at Barry.

'Ah, the proprietor!' Horace beamed. 'Where, prithee, would I locate the books

about myself?'

The librarian raised an eyebrow. 'You are …?'

Horace spluttered indignantly.

'Look, Horace, we can search for books about you over here,' I interrupted quickly, and dragged him to a computer.

'Er, nothing's coming up,' I told him, tapping at the keys.

'Preposterous! Have you spelt "Nincompoop" correctly?' Horace peered at the screen and tried to jab at the computer.

'Sir! I am going to have to ask you to leave the library unless you keep quiet!' hissed the librarian, striding over to us again.

Fortunately, Horace seemed to have had enough of the library. 'No good. These dandiprats don't know history from hornpipes! Onwards!'

I trotted after him, whispering apologies to all the people glaring at us, and wondered if my day could get ANY more embarrassing …

THE SECOND MIDDLE BIT

Yes, of course it could. I had Horace with me.

As we sat down for a rest near the playground, I heard a beeping.

'Unusual Damsel,' Horace began.

'*Harriet*,' I corrected, through gritted teeth.

'I have received some intelligence.'

I glanced over. He had a mobile phone!

'Horace, where on earth did you get that from?' I asked.

'Your grandfather gave it to me lest

we run into
peril. He is
communicating!'

A text message
had appeared on
the screen:

Hope all is well.
Your mum is
driving me mad.
Over.

Horace chuckled.

'I have encountered many souls using
these in Princes Park,' he remarked,
examining the phone delightedly. 'Let us
capture a selfie!'

He held the phone up in front of our

 66

faces and clicked inexpertly.

And it was at that moment I heard a familiar voice. A whiny, annoying, familiar voice I would rather not EVER hear.

'*HARRIET*? Is that YOU? What on earth are you doing, and who is *that*?'

It was Angela Spicklicket. And, like always, she had her giggling gang behind her.

'Who is that?' she repeated, walking towards us and pointing at Horace. 'Is that your dad?'

Her friends all giggled.

'Er, no,' I said. 'Angela, this is Horace.'

I didn't want to introduce them, but Angela was staring expectantly at me, and I needed to stop Horace jabbing at the phone before he managed to call someone.

Horace beamed at Angela and held out his hand. 'An ally, eh?

Pleasure to make your acquaintance, Mademoiselle!'

More giggling.

Angela looked at Horace's outstretched hand in disgust, as though it were covered in maggots.

'Ma-de-*what*?' she asked Horace, with one eyebrow raised. 'Do you, like, talk *normally*?'

More giggling.

'Horace, she's not exactly an ally,' I muttered to him. 'We should go.'

'Off so *soon*, Harriet?' asked Angela, in a nasty voice. 'I was just about to ask you where you got your *lovely* T-shirt from.'

Lots more giggling.

'Come on, Horace,' I said, and walked away. Horace frowned, but followed.

We'd only gone a few steps when suddenly I heard a loud *shriek*. I whipped my head around to see Angela, looking horrified, with a massive pigeon poo running down her nose! I was the one who giggled then. Angela howled and flapped

her arms and demanded that someone 'wipe up the mess THIS SECOND!'

Then Barry came flapping over and landed on Horace's hat. I stared at them both. I was pretty sure I could see a mischievous look in Barry's eyes …

'Shall we continue?' asked Horace innocently.

I grinned, and we continued.

THE LAST MIDDLE BIT

It turned out to be REALLY hard to please Horace.

After checking out the train station (too noisy), the playground (too small), and the bank (he got escorted off the premises – THAT was embarrassing), I was running out of places to suggest.

I thought about calling in on Megan and Fraser to ask them for some help ... but I wasn't sure whether my friends were ready for Horace. I wasn't sure anybody was.

'My Affable Accomplice, I fail to see any establishment that outshines the Silverbottom mansion,' said Horace. 'We shall simply have to ... FITZGIBBERS!' he suddenly exclaimed.

We were outside The Brim, a café that Mum and I went to only when it was A Super-Special Occasion, like my birthday, or when Mum needed A Nice Sit-Down and a Coffee.

Horace was peering at a plate that a waitress was carrying. 'That is a sandwich!' he announced.

'Er, yes,' I agreed, aware that people were staring at us. Again.

'I have spent YEARS watching

townsfolk eat sandwiches! Let us have one!
But make it larger, fifty times as large!'
Horace boomed at the waitress, who
frantically scrabbled for her notepad. 'We
need a sandwich fit for Lord Commander
Horatio—'

'Yes, yes, I think they get you!' I dragged him outside the café, my face as red as a tomato.

Horace plonked himself down on a bench to wait for his sandwich.

'AAARRRGHHHH!' Horace was so

heavy that a poor woman who was sitting at the other end was flung into the air.

Once I had helped retrieve the woman's

 76

shopping bags, I scuttled back to the bench. My face was now as red as two tomatoes.

'This looks DIVINE,' cried Horace, when his sandwich arrived. 'You are not partaking, Gentlewoman?'

'I don't have enough money,' I answered, my tummy rumbling.

'Money? I don't need money!' scoffed Horace, before taking a huge bite.

I stared at him. 'Are you telling me that you don't have any way to pay for your sandwich?'

And it was at that *very* moment the owner of the café came outside to clear

some tables.

'Sir!' she said, rather sharply. 'Did I hear that correctly? You have no way to pay for your sandwich?!'

Horace looked at me. I looked at him. All the customers at other tables looked at both of us.

I frantically scrabbled in my pockets, but came up with only 37p and an old piece of chewing gum.

Just as my face was going as red as 500 tomatoes, and the manager was Banning Us from Ever Returning to her Establishment, I saw Grandad's friend, Ned. He'd been having a coffee and had seen the whole thing and was now offering to pay for Horace's sandwich.

I gratefully took the money and double-promised to pay him back as soon as Pocket Money Day arrived. Then I dragged Horace away from the café. He was still happily munching.

'Look, Horace, I don't know where else
to suggest!' I told him as we walked away.
'You're going to HAVE to go back to your
pillar. We've tried everywhere else!'

It was getting close to teatime. I had to
go back home.

Horace raised a finger. 'Nay, we have *not*
tried everywhere else …'

'Look, we CAN'T invade the
Silverbottom mansion, Horace!' I insisted.
'What about the dogs?'

Horace took a deep breath. 'Yes. Well.
I have decided to face my fears … and
allow Barry to distract the hounds whilst
I topple Cuthbert from his pillar.'

Barry looked alarmed and ruffled his
feathers nervously.

'As for now, it is late. We do not invade after dark like common larcenists! We need rest. I shall reside another night in The Shed; then, on the morrow, we invade the Silverbottom mansion!'

I groaned.

THE EIGHTH BIT

The next morning I woke up early, opened the curtains really slowly, and crossed my fingers AND my toes that Horace hadn't done anything else to the shed.

I dashed outside.

'*Horace!*'

'My fine young companion, what cheer?'
said Horace, sipping tea on the balcony
with Barry.

The shed had a balcony. And a moat.
Mum was going to go nuts. And where
did the tea come from?

Just then Grandad came outside with his
paper and a slice of toast.

'Ah,' he said, when he saw the shed.
'Horace, er, still here then?'

I nodded.

Grandad looked at me. 'Listen, Harri,
I do want to help a fellow out, but I was
hoping to have my shed back today.'

He glanced back at the house, looking
miserable. 'Your mum made me help out

with doggy aerobics yesterday, you see, and I'm not sure I can take another day of it!'

I felt terrible. Grandad did LOADS to help me and Mum, and all he asked for was A Bit of Peace and Quiet In His Shed.

'I know, Grandad, I'm sorry,' I said. 'We searched EVERYWHERE—'

'Not quite everywhere,' Horace piped up from the balcony.

'And nowhere seemed right—' I continued.

'*Somewhere* still seems very right,' Horace interjected.

'And he won't go back to his pillar—'

'I certainly will NOT!'

Then suddenly we heard the sound of the back door opening.

Grandad and I looked at each other, horrified.

Mum!

'Horace, hide!' I hissed.

Mum was dressed in her yoga clothes and was humming a tune to herself. The tune came to an abrupt halt when she saw the shed. Her mouth opened. And then closed. And then opened again. It was quite interesting to watch.

'What,' she said softly (softly was ALWAYS the worst), 'has happened to the shed?'

'Ah, yes. Morning, Jennifer,' said Grandad, clearing his throat. 'I, er … decided to upgrade a little!'

Mum looked at the shed. 'There are *cannons.*'

'Yes,' said Grandad.

'And a *lifeboat,*' said Mum.

'Is there? I mean—yes,' said Grandad.

I felt double terrible then. Grandad was taking all the blame!

'When did you get all this *done*, exactly?' asked Mum.

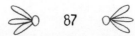

Grandad looked at me.

And at that VERY moment … a mobile phone started to ring. Oh no. Mum looked confused, and then followed the sound of the ringing around the side of the shed to

where Horace was hiding.

I cringed. 'Mum, I can explain …'

'And there's a ridiculous *statue* around the back of the shed!' she shrieked. 'This is not in keeping with the garden *AT ALL*. No, no, it'll have to go back. Today! Immediately!'

Mum glared at Grandad.

Grandad looked at me.

I looked at Horace.

Horace raised his eyebrows.

It looked as though we were off to the Silverbottom mansion.

THE BIT NEAR THE END

Once we were on our way, I decided to have a word with Horace.

'Horace, you've got us in a LOT of trouble,' I told him, as we walked side by side.

'Why, I am not afraid of trouble!' scoffed Horace.

'You can't just invade things whenever you like!' I continued.

It was quite fun telling someone off. No wonder grown-ups do it all the time.

'The duck house, Grandad's shed, the museum, the cinema, the library …' I

 90

ticked off everywhere we'd visited on my fingers.

(I barely had enough fingers.)

'And now Mayor Silverbottom's house,' I finished. 'They aren't yours, Horace! You need to go back to your pillar!'

Horace stopped.

He'd stopped to listen to me! I'd got through to him! Nope. He'd stopped because we'd reached the end of the long drive at the Silverbottom mansion.

The end of the long drive where there were quite unfriendly signs saying things like 'Very private' and 'Only visit with appointment, and even then I don't really want to see you' and 'Seriously, please go away'.

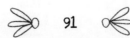

'OK, Horace,' I said nervously, 'these signs mean that we can't actually invade without an appointment. We should probably—'

'A stealth attack is best here!' interrupted Horace, totally ignoring my VERY SENSIBLE warning. He started stretching as if he were warming up for

a marathon. 'Follow my lead!' He began sort of zigzagging up the driveway, hiding behind various plants and bushes on the way.

Really unsuccessfully hiding, if you ask me.

I sighed (yet again) and caught up with Horace at the gates.

'Just look at Cuthbert's statue standing there,' he seethed, 'with his big pillar and his … his … STUPID FACE.'

'Shh!' I hissed. 'The guard dogs might come! We shouldn't—' Suddenly there were noises behind us. My knees went wobbly.

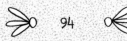

Someone was coming up the driveway! 'Quick, hide!' I whispered frantically, and squeezed behind a plant pot.

'*Hide?*' spluttered Horace.

'Yes! It's probably Mayor Silverbottom, and we're on his land!' I hissed, peeking through some leaves.

Horace looked grumpy and held a branch in front of his face.

Through the leaves, I could make out Mayor Silverbottom striding up the driveway, with three unhappy members of staff trudging behind him.

'Well, really, it's ridiculous to expect me to deal with this,' Mayor Silverbottom was saying, in his posh nasal voice, 'when I'm picking up the dogs from the grooming salon *and* having my toenails filed at 4 p.m.!'

One of his staff opened his mouth to speak, but Mayor Silverbottom talked over him.

'We've arranged the competition—with money that could have been spent repairing my swimming pool, I'll have you know—to satisfy members of the *public*.' Mayor Silverbottom seemed to struggle over this last word, as if it left a nasty taste in his mouth. 'And to be honest, good riddance to that giant stone oaf.'

He tapped a long number into a keypad, the gate swung open, and he marched towards the house.

'Will you PLEASE hurry up?' he barked over his shoulder.

His staff scurried nervously behind him,

98

weighed down by briefcases and shopping and huge stacks of papers.

I saw Barry quietly flap overhead and pinch one of the papers from the top of the pile.

Mayor Silverbottom and his staff didn't glance towards me or Horace, but I didn't want to breathe until the front door had slammed safely shut behind them. (Even though I was probably purple in the face.)

Barry immediately flew over and dropped the paper into my hand.

I peered at it:

My mouth fell open.

'Er, Horace,' I began, 'you might want to have a look at this.'

Horace came out from behind his branch and looked at the flyer. 'Juggling jitterbugs. Does this refer to *my* pillar?' He looked up, amazed. 'But, but ... this is MY pillar!'

'What do you think—' I started.

'NO PREVIOUS EXPERIENCE NECESSARY?' roared Horace. 'Outrageous! Are they oblivious to the *expertise* that goes into standing on a pillar?'

He looked rather hurt.

'These villains cannot give my pillar to somebody else! Perchance I've had misgivings along the way … but it belongs to me. It's my HOME.'

I stopped myself from sighing or rolling my eyes. (It was HARD.) Instead I patted Horace on the arm. 'This is what I've been telling you,' I said gently. 'You can't just take something that belongs to somebody else!'

 101

Horace looked up at Mayor Silverbottom's house, with its fancy gates and rows of windows.

He took a deep breath and narrowed his eyes, looking as if he'd made up his mind about something. 'Devoted Allies,' began Horace, addressing me and Barry. 'I have made up my mind about something.'

(Told you.)

'I do believe it is time …'

'Yes?' I said, holding my breath.

'… to return …' said Horace, puffing out his chest.

'Yes?' I squeaked, still trying to hold my breath.

'… to my rightful home,' finished Horace. 'As long as I stand, I will defend

my home until the end. There will be no scoundrels invading *my* pillar! To Princes Park!' he cried, and charged back down the driveway towards the town.

'Yes!' I whooped in delight, and charged back down the driveway after Horace.

THE ALMOST
LAST BIT

Sure enough, as we arrived at Princes Park, we could see people trying out for the pillar position.

Each person was allowed a few minutes to demonstrate their skill at standing still, while two of Mayor Silverbottom's staff watched and took notes.

As competitions go, it was really quite boring.

We watched, hidden in the bushes at the edge of the park, as various people wobbled on the pillar.

Mum's yoga teacher did a super-cool pose on one leg with her arms all twisted but then fell off.

The man who owned the pet shop had a go, but he had a parrot, three hamsters, and a chihuahua with him, and they wouldn't stay still.

Lord Commander Horatio Frederick Wellington Nincompoop Maximus Pimpleberry the Third

PILLAR TRY-OUTS
COURTESY OF
Mayor Silverbottom

Lord Commander Horatio Frederick Wellington Nincompoop Maximus Pimpleberry the Third

I even saw my friend
Megan having a go!
But she was afraid of
heights so only managed
about four seconds.

Horace was spluttering
with indignation. 'They
haven't mastered the
correct poses! They
don't even wear hats and
medals, the incompetent
buffoons!'

Lord Commander Horatio Frederick Wolfington Nincompoop Maximus Pimpleberry the Third

After seeing a few more entrants, Horace couldn't take it any longer.

'A surprise attack!' he declared, doing his warm-up stretches again. 'Without further ado! I shall amass the troops—Barry! Barry, come hither! You shall take the north of the park. And you,' he continued, pointing at me, 'shall prepare your largest sword and invade from the south.'

Horace paused. 'You *do* carry a sword, I presume?'

'Or,' I said slowly, 'how about we just distract them, and you can nip back on to the pillar?'

'Distract them?' asked Horace, looking disappointed. 'No invasions? No swords? Not a custard pie thrown?'

'No,' I said firmly. 'Just a distraction, and *I* have got JUST the plan.'

While the contestants were helping an elderly woman down from the pillar, I did some Super-Stealthy Creeping along the edge of the park.

When I reached the gate, I took a deep breath and in my loudest voice shouted, 'OH MY GOODNESS, THE PARK KIOSK IS SELLING CHOCOLATE BISCUITS! MAYOR SILVERBOTTOM MUST HAVE UNBANNED THEM AT LAST!'

The people by the pillar turned around

sharper than you could say … well,
'chocolate biscuits'.

'Chocolate?'

'Biscuits?'

'*Chocolate biscuits?*'

There was an immediate stampede
towards the kiosk.

I crept back to Horace, grinning.

'Why, exceptional work, soldier!' said

Horace. 'Fine distraction technique! You have learnt that from me.'

I rolled my eyes.

Horace strolled over to his pillar and threw away the 'PILLAR TRY-OUTS' sign. He brushed away a few specks of dirt and gazed at the pillar fondly. 'Undoubtedly the finest spot in town,' he said, heaving himself back on to the top. 'Cuthbert

doesn't know what he's missing, the old poltroon!'

Even Barry rolled his eyes this time.

'I shall stay to guard the area,' said Horace, settling back into position, 'lest those rapscallions try any more chicanery! Can't trust them at all. You will … pay me another visit soon, Peculiar Child?' Horace asked.

I grimaced. 'My NAME is … Oh, forget it,' I said. 'Yes, I will. Someone had better check up on you. Who *knows* what trouble you'll get into next.'

I looked up at Horace and thought about

how this ridiculous statue had suddenly caused so much chaos in my life.

Barry flew up and landed on Horace's head. He raised his wing in a wave.

'Well, bye, then,' I said. I strolled away with my hands in my pockets. Obviously I felt *very* relieved now that Horace was back where he belonged and out of trouble. But suddenly, weirdly, I felt a bit lonely.

'Jolly good!' called Horace after me. 'Oh, and one more thing …'

I paused and braced myself.

'Thank you,' he said. 'Thank you, Harri.'

I stopped, completely startled at hearing my name. Harri. It was what my *friends* called me. I turned back, gave him a final grin, and ran off home.

 114

THE ACTUAL LAST BIT

So, life is actually a bit better since I got to know Lord Commander Horatio Frederick Wallington Nincompoop Maximus Pimpleberry the Third.

Grandad decided to keep his shed just as Horace left it.

Mum wasn't too happy about it, but she's pretty busy with her doggy aerobics classes now. She even said we might be able to get a puppy of our own, which would be Totally Awesome! (Maybe don't tell Horace.)

Angela Spicklicket hasn't talked to me AT ALL since the day she met Horace and Barry, and that's JUST the way I like it. She also seems a bit nervous of pigeons now …

Grandad and I go and check on Horace quite a bit. He seems happy. He sends Barry off to get him sandwiches.

Everyone else in the town seems pretty pleased to have Horace back where he belongs. As far as I know, no one has graffitied him, or put a traffic cone on his head, or dropped litter on him, or annoyed him at all.

So, everything seems to have worked out for the better.

Oh. Except for …

'THOSE DASTARDLY PIGEONS!'

THE (ACTUAL) END

 117

HORACE'S DICTIONARY

Sometimes I have no idea what Horace is talking about, so I thought we should include these explanations of some of his funny expressions. Horace agreed and said, 'I have provided some assistance, in case any of you young whippersnappers have any trouble with my words!'

ACQUIESCENT accepting, not likely to argue or disagree with me.

AFFABLE pleasant and friendly. Rather like Barry.

AMASS gather together, get a large amount of. For example: *I rather like to amass sandwiches.*

CHICANERY trickery.

COMPATRIOT a fellow citizen. Harriet's fine grandfather is a compatriot.

DANDIPRAT someone young or not worth bothering with.

FITZGIBBERS an exclamation of surprise, of my own creation. For example: *Fitzgibbers! Doesn't Cuthbert have a large nose!*

FOOT SOLDIER someone who does terribly important work but who is not as important as me. (To me, of course, most people are foot soldiers.)

FORTH onwards. For example: *From this day forth, I shall always protect my pillar.* Not to be confused with fourth, which comes after third. Which comes after second. Which …

GENTLEWOMAN a fine, noble woman. Some might say this is a bit old-fashioned now.

HENCEFORTH from this moment in time. For example: *Henceforth, I shall always agree Horace is correct.*

HITHER towards a place. For example: *When the park attendant saw his sunken pedalo, it brought him hither.*

ILLUSTRIOUS well known and remarkable. (Somewhat like me.)

LARCENIST a thief.

LEST to try and prevent.

MADEMOISELLE a polite French word to address a woman. Similar to 'Miss' in English.

MAN-AT-ARMS a soldier.

MORROW the following day. You might use tomorrow. But I prefer morrow.

NAY no.

PERCHANCE perhaps. For example: *My pillar, perchance, is much better than the Silverbottom mansion.*

POLTROON a coward.

PRITHEE a polite way of saying please. For example, if I were feeling polite, I might say to the pigeons: *Prithee, would you stop fouling my head?*

PREPOSTEROUS similar to ridiculous, impossible, or outrageous.

PROPRIETOR the owner of the business or property. For example: *Harriet's grandfather is the proprietor of his cannon shed.*

RAPSCALLION a mischievous individual.

STERLING this can refer to British money, but I use the word to describe an excellent thing or person.

THENCEFORTH from this moment in time (like henceforth), or it could mean, from this place or this point onwards. For example: *Thenceforth those dandiprats never covered me in graffiti ever again.*

THRICE three times.

TOME a book, especially a large one with lots of words.

WHIPPERSNAPPER a young person who might not know everything. Definitely not a fish.

YONDER at some distance over there. For example: *Look yonder! There is Princes Park, home to the finest statue in all the land.*

ZARBLES an expression of surprise, of my own creation. For example: *Zarbles! This word is a bit like Fitzgibbers!*

LOVE HORACE AND HARRIET?
WHY NOT TRY THESE TOO!